Acorn
and
Button

Laura Petrisin

Copyright © 2022 Laura Petrisin

To my mother-in-law, Do, who always believed in me.

Print ISBN: 978-1-958877-52-4

Published by BookLocker.com, Inc., Trenton, Georgia.

BookLocker.com, Inc.
2022

First Edition

Chapter 1
The Meeting

Acorn was a small nut who lived in a big woods. Most acorns were content to hang from trees or lay motionless on the ground. But, Acorn was different. He wanted to explore the woods and make friends.

It was a warm Autumn morning. Leaves were just starting to change from green to crimson and gold. Acorn was strolling through the forest when he came across a button standing on the path.

Acorn stopped and stared. "Hello!" he said. "Are you a nut? I haven't seen your kind around here before."

Button did not care to be called a nut, and snorted, "No, I am not a nut, Sir! I am a button."

"Well, where do you come from?" asked Acorn, puzzled. "I come from that big oak tree over to your left."

Button began to think Acorn was too nosy for his own good.

"Not that it is any of your business, but I come from a sewing basket," he said. "The basket was dropped on the way to town and I bounced out."

This seemed a bit odd to Acorn, but he was too polite to say anything. "What is that sticking out of your middle?" he asked. "A branch?"

"A branch!" shouted Button. "What impertinence, Sir! That is a needle or, to be more precise, a sword! I will teach you not to insult me!" Button drew the needle from his belt, lifted it high above his head, and cried, "En garde!"

He chased Acorn around a tree three times, huffing and puffing. Then, just as Acorn began to tire, Button tripped over his own feet and fell. He landed with the needle stuck

into the ground and his feet dangling in the air. He couldn't pull the needle out of the ground and he was too afraid to let go of it.

"Look at the mess you've gotten me into!" Button thundered at Acorn. "Come help me, you scoundrel!"

Acorn was hiding behind the tree and was ready to run home. He'd had enough of Button! But then he noticed that Button was blinking his eyes very fast as if trying not to cry.

Acorn came out from behind the tree and walked slowly up to Button.

"I didn't mean to hurt your feelings," he said.

"Well, you have," Button complained. "You've wounded me to the core and now I'm stuck."

"I think I can fix that," Acorn responded.

Acorn gave the needle one good kick. The needle flew up in the air, and Button landed on his feet. He stood looking at the ground for a moment, and then gave out a small cough.

"You're not such a bad sort, really," said Button. "You just need someone to teach you manners. Hmm... I wonder who's available?"

Acorn waited while Button thought hard. Suddenly, Button grinned and said, "Why, I can teach you! I'm an expert on manners. Come with me."

"Thank you," said Acorn as he walked beside Button. "I didn't know I needed any manners. You're very kind."

"Manners can be tricky, but I have it down to a science," Button explained. "First of all, never talk when your mouth is full of mashed potatoes and blueberries. I witnessed that once, and was ill for days."

Acorn felt a little sick himself at the thought of it.

"Also, when you want to interrupt someone who's speaking, shout 'excuse me' very loudly in their ear. That should stop the chatter."

Acorn nodded, but looked confused. "I have a lot to learn," he thought.

"Do you like to explore, Button?" Acorn asked.

"Why, I am an expert on exploration! I've traveled the world," said Button.

Acorn brightened. "Do you think we could go exploring together some time?"

"I don't see why not," replied Button. "But, right now, I must find a new home."

He stopped, and looked around. "These woods aren't so bad as far as woods go."

"I know a tree that has a hole in its trunk," said Acorn. "It's close to the ground and looks cozy."

Button smiled. "You don't say! Hmm... Let's take a look. I may stick around here for a while."

Acorn gave a happy skip. He had a friend to explore with!

CHAPTER 2

Treasure

One morning, Acorn strolled along the forest path and spied a piece of paper peeking up from the grass. He picked it up. There was writing with arrows and drawings of rocks and trees. At the bottom was a skull and bones.

"This looks important!" exclaimed Acorn and ran off to show Button. Button was waking up when he heard his friend call.

"Hello, Button! Come see what I found!" Acorn stood outside, waving the paper. Button hurried over to look.

"What is it?" asked Acorn.

"Have you never seen a treasure map before?" Button asked. "Surely you know about pirates, and treasure chests, and ships on the high seas!"

"I've never seen a high sea," answered Acorn.

Button grabbed the map. "This will lead us to hidden treasure. A pirate probably dropped it during a rampage."

Button examined the map and read out loud, "Start at walnut tree. Go east to big rock by pond. Then, go south to stream where you will see an old tree stump. The treasure is in there!"

"We've no time to waste!" cried Button, "Off to the walnut tree!"

Acorn and Button arrived at the tree and then walked east to the pond. There was no big rock in sight. They circled the pond twice before discovering it half hidden in some tall grass. Then, they turned south in search of the stream. It took a long time to find it. Acorn and Button had never seen the stream before. They were about to give up and go home when they heard the gentle rippling of water. Right in front of them, next to the stream, stood an old, rotting stump.

Button peered into the top of the stump and gasped. He reached in and pulled out a dirty, white handkerchief. It was tied in a knot and obviously held something. Acorn helped Button lay it on the ground and they opened it. Then, Button kicked his feet in the air.

"We hit the jackpot, Acorn! These are rare treasures!" cried Button. Spread before them was a white feather, a red marble, two bottle caps, half of a robin's egg, a rusty key, and a tiny, smooth, silver stone.

Button slid the needle out from his belt and placed it on the ground. He slid the white feather where the needle had been and strutted. "How do I look, Acorn?" Button asked.

Acorn said, "You look like an admiral." Then he crouched down to admire the tiny, silver stone.

"That will make a fine addition to your pebble collection," Button commented.

Acorn smiled, and replied, "It's just the right size."

Right then, they heard voices surprisingly close. "How could you lose the map, Sammy?" someone asked in an angry tone.

"Pirates! Run for your life!" cried Button.

Acorn immediately ran for cover behind a big rock. Button, however, was so agitated that he ran in circles until he became dizzy and fell to the ground.

At that moment, two young raccoon cubs appeared. One was larger than the other and a little older. The smaller raccoon wore a red bandana on his head and the bigger one had a black hat with cross bones. They stopped in their tracks when they saw the handkerchief on the ground.

"Hey, someone broke into our treasure, Clyde!" sputtered the smaller racoon.

"I told you to call me Captain Mad Dog," the bigger racoon retorted. He checked the objects on the handkerchief. "Looks like the scalawags didn't take anything except for the feather, Sammy."

Hearing that, Button lay very still on the ground.

"There it is," said Sammy. "It got stuck in a button!"

Clyde walked over, pulled out the feather, and tossed Button high into the air.

Button flipped head over heels, and landed near the rock Acorn was hiding behind.

"Why did you do that, Clyde...I mean, Captain Mad Dog?" asked Sammy. "We could have put it in our treasure."

Clyde scoffed. "Who wants that old thing? It's just a button."

In spite of his dizziness, Button jumped to his feet. "JUST a button? Did that ruffian say JUST a button?!" Button looked around wildly. "Where is my sword?" he thundered. "That villain will regret mocking me!"

Button took a step forward and then felt himself grabbed from behind.

"Shhhhhh... Button." Acorn whispered, holding his friend tightly. "Be quiet. Maybe they won't see us."

Button struggled to get loose. "Let go, Acorn! They shall see the point of my blade! Let go, I say! YIKES!"

Button and Acorn were suddenly lifted far above the ground. "I found the button," said Sammy, "and an acorn right next to it. I'm putting them in our treasure!"

Clyde shrugged. "Have it your way. Tie up everything, and put it back. We better get going before Ma starts looking for us."

The racoons tied up the handkerchief with Acorn and Button inside. Then, they placed it in the tree stump and left.

Button and Acorn lay still. It was quiet and very dark. Finally, Acorn stirred. "What do we do now, Button?"

"If only I had my sword," Button replied, "I would rip our way out of here."

Suddenly, Acorn heard a scratching sound. "Do you hear that, Button?"

Button listened. It sounded like claws climbing up the side of the stump. Next, they heard cloth tear. Then, they saw big, sharp teeth poke through a hole in the handkerchief.

"Dragons!" cried Button. "Hide underneath the bottle caps!"

There was no time. The handkerchief began to shake violently, and the pieces of treasure tumbled out, including Button and Acorn.

Acorn lay stunned on the ground. When he opened his eyes, he was staring into the face of a large squirrel. Any nut knows that the acorn is a favorite on a squirrel's menu. Acorn gulped, and prepared for the worst.

Button lay on his stomach several feet away, but he managed to lift his head. To his horror, he saw the ferocious beast towering over Acorn. Luckily, he also saw his lost sword a foot away.

Button leapt to his feet, grabbed the sword, and ran toward the beast. The squirrel had Acorn in its paws and was lifting him to its mouth.

"Oh no you don't, vermin!" yelled Button. He vaulted in the air using his sword as a pole and pricked the squirrel's nose with it. The squirrel dropped Acorn, shook its head vigorously, and scurried off. Acorn lay still on the ground.

"Come now, my valiant comrade, wake up!" Button said. But, there was no response. Tears welled up in Button's eyes. "Wake up, Acorn, we must tell of our adventures! We have escaped pirates and fought dragons!"

Acorn, who had fainted, opened his eyes. "And, I was almost gobbled up," he said.

"Until I saved you!" cried Button, with surprise and joy. He pulled Acorn up by the hand.

"We will record this day in our journals, Acorn. It has been an adventure of the highest sort!"

Then, the two tired friends headed for their homes, forgetting entirely about the treasure.

CHAPTER 3

Acorn's Art

Acorn woke up in a creative mood. He wanted to draw something, but he didn't know what. He got a pencil and sketch pad and headed outdoors. Hearing the sound of birds, Acorn looked up to see three chickadees chirping on a branch overhead.

Acorn sat down by a rock and started to sketch the chickadees. After a few minutes, one of the birds noticed him. "What are you doing, Acorn?" the chickadee asked.

"I am sketching you and your friends," answered Acorn. "I hope you don't mind."

The chickadees were quite flattered by this. "Oh no, we don't mind!" they cried. They preened their feathers, puffed out their chests, and sat still as Acorn drew.

Finally, Acorn said, "Done!" He put down his pencil.

The birds couldn't wait to see the drawing! They flew down to take a peek at the sketch pad in Acorn's hands. There was a moment of shocked silence, and then the first chickadee spoke in a shrill.

"Why, that looks nothing like me! I'm sleek, not fluffy!"

The next chickadee chimed in. "You made my beak much too long! I am known far and wide for my dainty beak!"

Then all the birds began to laugh at Acorn. "Who taught you to draw anyway?" they said. "You call yourself an artist?".

The chickadees laughed until their bellies hurt and then they flew away.

Acorn looked at his drawing. Then, he tore it from his pad, dropped it to the ground, and slowly walked home.

Later that day, Button was enjoying his afternoon stroll when he came across Acorn's drawing on the ground. "Why, what is this?" Button wondered as he picked up the paper and looked at it.

"Perhaps an art collector dropped it!" Button peered at the drawing again. No signature. He scratched his head. "I must find a way to return this piece of fine art to its owner."

Button got an idea, and hurried home. He found a crayon and a piece of cardboard and began to make a sign. It said:

Found!
An original drawing of birds on a tree branch!
If you want it back, contact Button!

"There!" declared Button. "This sign is ready to hang on a tree. Now, where are my hammer and nails?" He found his hammer but could not find his nails, no matter how hard he searched.

"I'll go to Acorn's house," he decided, "and see if he has a nail I can borrow."

When Button arrived at Acorn's house, he showed Acorn his sign and asked, "Do you have a nail for this sign, Acorn?"

Acorn read the sign and looked confused. He asked, "Where did you find the drawing, Button?"

"Not far from here," answered Button, "I have the drawing with me. I'll show you."

Button handed the drawing to Acorn. Acorn stared at the paper and said, "I drew this, Button, but it's not very good and I threw it away."

"Threw it away?" thundered Button. "Good heavens! Are you in your right mind, Sir?"

Button snatched the drawing from Acorn, and waved it. "This is art! Art is meant to be displayed, not thrown away!"

Acorn took a step back. "I didn't know it was art. You may have it if you'd like, Button."

This calmed Button considerably. "May I?" he asked in an awed voice. "I know just where I'll put it - in my study. I'll have it framed, but first, you must sign it, Acorn. Here's my crayon."

While Acorn was signing his name, Button remarked, "I didn't know you had such talent, my friend."

Acorn shook his head a little. "I didn't know, either."

CHAPTER 4
A New Friend

Button looked outside and sighed. "I'm bored," he muttered. It had been bitterly cold for two weeks, shutting him in. But, now the sun shone, and there was a thaw in the air. "I wonder if Acorn is bored, too?" He decided to put his rubber boots on and see if Acorn was in the mood to go for a walk.

Luckily, Acorn was quite excited to get out too, and the friends headed down the path leading to the apple orchard. The apples were long gone because the deer had been feasting on them since fall.

When they got to the orchard, they stood beneath a tree and watched a couple of young rabbits chase each other in the fading snow. As they watched, something dripped on Button's head. Then, he felt another drip. Looking up, Button could see he was standing beneath a long icicle hanging from a branch.

"Good grief," Button said, and moved away. "Are you crying, Miss?" He asked the icicle.

"No, Sir. I'm melting," answered Icicle. She was slender and graceful, and the reflection from the sky gave her a lovely bluish hue.

Icicle cried out suddenly, "I'm falling, and will break!" With that, Icicle lost her grip on the branch and plunged downward. Acorn and Button rushed over in the nick of time and Button caught her in his arms. Icicle looked up at Button. "You saved me," she whispered.

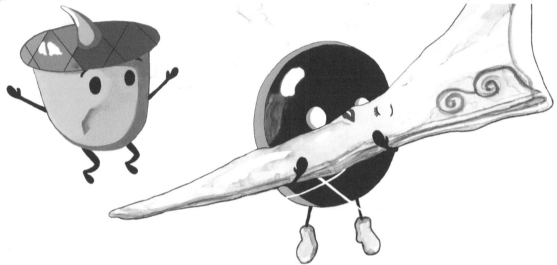

Button carried Icicle to the tree, and leaned her gently against it.

"Can you walk?" Acorn asked.

"Oh no," replied Icicle with a laugh. "I can't walk. I just hang from this or that branch during the winter months, growing longer and more beautiful."

"You are very beautiful," agreed Button.

"Please don't interrupt," said Icicle. She continued, "Then, when the season changes and warmer winds begin to blow, I melt little by little until I disappear."

Acorn looked distraught. "Disappear?" he asked.

"Say it isn't so!" Button exclaimed.

"But, it is so," said Icicle in a practical tone.

"We just found you and now we'll lose you," Button said sadly. A small tear fell from his eye. Next to him, Acorn sniffled.

Icicle laughed and her laugh was like the tinkle of bells. "Don't be silly. You will see me again when the north wind comes back next year, bringing the frost and the ice."

Button and Acorn still looked miserable and Icicle softened.

"Come sit by me, boys," she said. " We'll talk, and make jokes, and share riddles in the time we have left. I don't mind melting because I know that when I come back, I will be more beautiful than ever! That is the nature of icicles."

So, Button and Acorn sat beside Icicle. They shared riddles and told her the funniest jokes they knew. As they talked and laughed, Icicle grew smaller and smaller, and her laugh fainter and fainter until she was finally gone.

When Button and Acorn could no longer see or hear Icicle, they stood up and slowly walked home.

"I've never met anyone like Icicle," Button said as he shuffled along, looking at the ground.

"Me neither," agreed Acorn. "I liked her laugh."

"It was pure melody, my friend," Button sniffed.

Acorn glanced over. "We may see her again some day, Button."

But Button was quiet.

Soon, spring came
and burst out in
yellow daffodils and
unfurling tree buds.

Then, summer dawdled by with
fireflies
and long, lazy days.

Finally, Autumn arrived and
frosted the ground where the
orange pumpkins grew.

Button woke up one morning to find the ground, trees, and bushes covered in a newly fallen snow. The sun shone, the sky was blue, and the snow sparkled. Button decided to call on Acorn and go for a walk.

The crisp air was invigorating! Rabbit tracks lay spread out before them. Button picked up his step and started to whistle. That's when they heard a familiar voice.

"Well now, boys, where are you off to?"

Button's heart swelled and Acorn grinned. They looked up to see Icicle hanging from a tree and looking more beautiful than ever.

CHAPTER 5

Lost

It was twilight - that magical time when a golden sun swings low and the first stars appear faintly in a darkening, purple sky. Button headed over to Acorn's house carrying an empty jar.

"Hello, Acorn!" he called from outside, "Would you care to join me in a firefly expedition?"

Acorn came to the door. "A firefly what?"

"Expedition, my friend!" Button boomed. "I'm hunting fireflies.

"What will you do with them after you catch them?" asked Acorn.

"I'll keep them in my house," replied Button, "where I can gaze upon their beauty whenever I want."

At that moment, a small firefly flew right by Button and Acorn. Button gave chase.

"What a specimen!" he shouted. "Come quickly, Acorn!"

Acorn followed as fast as he could. The firefly landed on a bush and Button crept up on it. But, just as he opened his jar, the firefly flew off again. This went on for quite a while.

Button and Acorn chased the firefly past the pond, through the apple orchard, and beyond the big boulder where they often had a picnic lunch. The forest grew darker as they ran, and Button suddenly tripped over a tree root, dropping his jar.

Acorn stopped, and asked anxiously, "Are you hurt, Button?"

Button stood up and brushed himself off. "No, I don't think so."

The two stood still and looked around. The firefly had disappeared. Night had fallen. Shadows loomed and clouds filled the sky.

Acorn gulped. "Do you know where we are, Button?"

Button peered at the trees outlined against the sky. He didn't recognize them. "I'm afraid I don't, Acorn."

Acorn trembled, and said, "We're lost!"

"If only we had a clear sky and stars," said Button. "The North Star would guide us home."

Hearing the word "home" gave Acorn a tight feeling in his throat. He thought of his comfortable bed made of twigs and a big, oak leaf.

"Do you think there are any wild animals around?" asked Acorn as he inched closer to Button.

"I dare say there are," answered Button. "Big, ferocious beasts that only come out at night may be watching us right now."

Just then, a twig cracked nearby. The two raccoon cubs, Clyde and Sammy, had been hunting for treasure and popped their heads above a nearby bush.

"Just as I feared!" Button shouted and grabbed Acorn's hand. "Run for your life!"

The coons watched Acorn and Button speed away.

"I didn't know buttons could run," said Clyde, scratching his head.

"Or acorns!" Sammy chimed in.

They returned to searching for treasure to add to their bounty.

Meanwhile, Acorn and Button ran and ran through the forest. Acorn stumbled once, but Button pulled him to his feet. Whenever they stopped to rest, the night sounds surrounded them. The hoot of an owl or a rustle in a bush filled them with fear, and they raced off again. They ran until their legs felt like jelly, and they could barely breathe.

Finally, Button stopped. "It's no use," he gasped. "We can't keep on. We will have to face the beasts..."

Button drew out his needle and stood in front of Acorn, who was trembling from head to foot. They waited...

Just then, every bush and tree surrounding the two friends lit up with hundreds of fireflies that were blinking and weaving about. The shadows lifted and there was no beast to be seen.

Acorn cried, "The fireflies have come to our rescue!"

There was a clear path before them, and they heard something very soft yet distinct, like the sigh of a breeze or the ripple of a stream. "Follow us," came a whisper.

The fireflies traveled slowly down the path, and Acorn and Button followed them until they recognized the big boulder where they always picnicked. They knew the rest of the way home.

With relief, Acorn began to thank the fireflies when they vanished suddenly, disappearing as quickly as they had appeared.

Button set off out down the path. "This way, Acorn," he said.

As they walked, Acorn noticed that Button's jar was missing. "Did you forget your jar, Button?" he asked.

"No," answered Button. "I left it back in the forest."

"Why did you do that?"

Button was quiet for a moment and then said. "Maybe fireflies don't like being chased. Maybe they don't like being stuck in a jar. I was stuck to a sleeve once and I didn't care for it."

Acorn nodded.

Button sighed. "To be honest, I regret my plan to capture fireflies for my own personal use."

Acorn thought about this. Then, he smiled at his friend. "But, I think you would have let them go, Button."

"Quite right," said Button, brightening and picking up his step.

The two walked on, and it wasn't long before they arrived home, safe and sound.

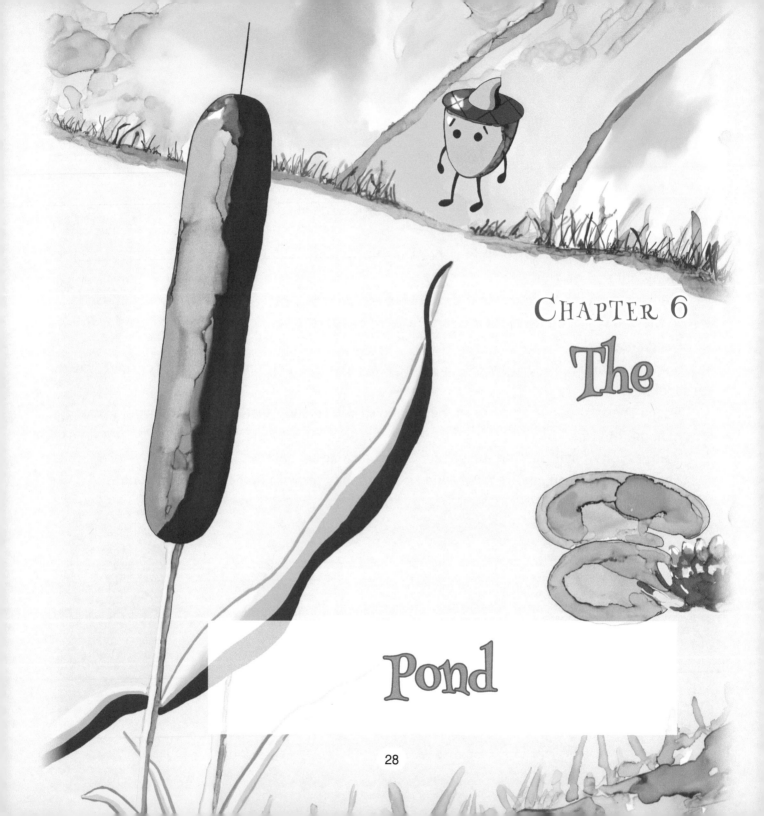

CHAPTER 6

The

Pond

The sun was so hot that birds fanned each other with their wings and squirrels lay like limp noodles over shaded tree branches. Worms tunneled deeper into the cool earth and frogs took mud baths in the thick, black goop.

Acorn walked slowly down a little grass path that led to a nearby pond. "Almost there," he said. He skipped when he saw the cattails standing strong and straight like sentinels at the pond's edge. Acorn ran toward the water, ready to somersault right in. "Here I go!" he shouted.

Suddenly the word "Halt!" rang out. Acorn stopped. The tallest cattail barred his way and towered above him. "Who goes there?"

Acorn's eyes got round and he squeaked, "Acorn."

"What's your business?" barked Cattail.

"Swimming?" answered Acorn.

"We had a couple of rowdy nuts here yesterday, teasing the turtles and disturbing the peace!" Cattail bent down to peer at Acorn. "Were you one of them?"

Acorn felt nervous. "No, Sir."

"Humph! Well, proceed and see that you behave yourself!" said Cattail.

Acorn gave a nod and quickly made his way past Cattail.

He waded into the pond and bobbed around. The water was refreshing and Acorn was practicing his back stroke when he heard a voice nearby.

"Hey, you! Pssssssst! Yeah, you. Over here." Acorn looked around, but he didn't see anyone.

"I'm here by the lily pad," whispered the voice.

Acorn looked over at a cluster of lily pads. Underneath the biggest was a walnut peeking out. Acorn swam over.

"Why are you hiding?" he asked the walnut.

"Keep it down!" hissed Walnut. "I was here yesterday having a little fun with my buddies and old Cattail threw us out of the pond."

Acorn didn't know what to make of this and kept quiet.

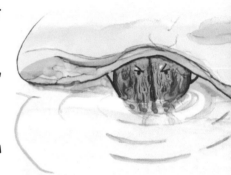

"I'm going to get even with him for ruining our fun," continued Walnut. "And, you're going to help me!"

Acorn gulped. "What are you going to do?"

"I'm gonna grab a big stick," replied Walnut. "Then, I'm gonna sneak up behind Cattail and give him a smack."

Acorn was horrified to hear this and stood paralyzed!

Walnut shoved him. "And, you're gonna distract ol' Rat Tail while I swim up behind him. Understand?"

Acorn started shaking. "How am I going to distract him?" he asked.

"I don't care how you do it, Corn Dog, you just make sure you do it!" Walnut pushed Acorn in the direction of Cattail. "And don't even think of running 'cause I'll chase you down and clobber you instead," he threatened. "Now, move it!"

Acorn walked toward Cattail feeling sick to his stomach. He was hardly friends with Cattail, but he didn't want to see him smacked! How could this happen? He was about to become an accomplice to a crime!

He'd have to find a way to warn Cattail without Walnut finding out. Acorn tried to come up with a plan, but it felt like everything was moving in slow motion and he couldn't think. He turned around and saw Walnut pick up a stick along the shoreline and wade back into the water.

Walnut noticed Acorn watching and waved the stick at him while drawing a finger across his throat at the same time.

Acorn continued walking, and as he got nearer, he could hear Cattail talking to himself.

"I don't know how they expect me to police this pond properly with so many hooligans around and no backup," Cattail muttered. He was getting ready to take his break when Acorn startled him. "Good grief!" he cried, "Where did you come from? You should never sneak up on a body like that!"

Acorn stood silent and Cattail asked, "What do you want? Speak up!"

But, Acorn couldn't speak. Behind Cattail, he saw Walnut holding the stick overhead and swimming nearer and nearer to the bank. The villain grinned wickedly.

Acorn tried to open his mouth, but nothing came out. He finally raised a finger and pointed toward the water.

Cattail turned around in time to see a large fish come up to the surface and swallow Walnut! "Good heavens!" He cried.

The fish disappeared, only to surface again a moment later. In the next instant, Walnut was sailing in the air overhead. The fish did not like the taste of Walnut and spit him out!

Walnut flew past Cattail and Acorn until he hit a beech tree with a loud crack! Acorn cringed because that is a sound no nut likes to hear. Walnut fell to the ground, split in two.

There was an awful silence, and then Walnut moved. Half of him stood up on one leg, grabbing his other half with one hand. Then, holding himself together with both hands, he ran for home.

Cattail recognized Walnut and shouted after him, "Yes, run, you ruffian, and don't come back!" He wondered, "What was that troublemaker up to?"

"He was getting ready to smack you," said Acorn.

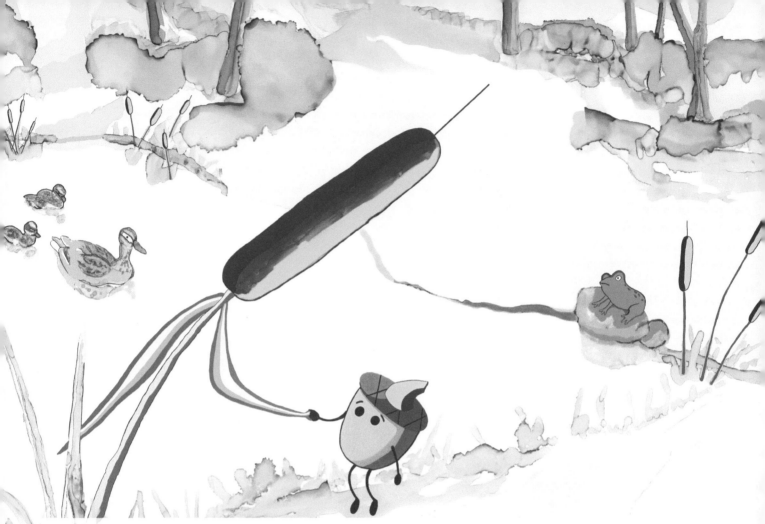

"Smack me?" repeated Cattail. "Well, he was the one who got smacked! Stay clear of nuts with questionable character, my friend." Cattail drew himself up tall and straight.

"And now, I am happy to inform you that because of your selfless act of bravery, you are eligible for a pass to swim in the pond any time you want!"

Acorn wasn't sure what he had done to earn this honor, but he smiled shyly and asked, "Could I bring my friend, Button?"

"Of course!" boomed Cattail, giving a gracious wave of his hand. "Bring anyone you'd like!"

With that, Acorn waved goodbye to Cattail and headed for Button's house to tell him the good news.

CHAPTER 7
A Dinner Party

The end of August arrived with shorter days and cooler evenings. Acorn and Button had used Acorn's free pass to the pond to swim on the hottest days during that summer. The two had gotten to be good friends with Cattail.

The morning sun was warm as Acorn stepped outside to check his mailbox. Inside the small, hollow log was a light green envelope. Acorn opened it and read the card:

You are invited to a dinner party hosted by Cattail.
Where: The pond.
When: Saturday at 4:30 p.m.
Be prompt!

"Why, that's tomorrow!" said Acorn, and he ran to Button's house.

Acorn showed the invitation to Button. "I have one, too," Button said. "Let's go to the dinner together, Acorn!"

The next day, Acorn and Button arrived at the pond at 4:30 sharp. A white, cloth napkin lay on the grass near the water. Placed neatly on the napkin were tiny bark plates with wild raspberries and tiny bark cups full of honeysuckle juice. Seated around the napkin were two red newts, a small, green frog, and four yellow finches. Cattail stood at the head of the group, waiting for the last arrivals. Acorn and Button quickly took their places.

Cattail spoke, "I have called you all here for an important occasion. Recently, I was almost assaulted by a ruffian named Walnut, who wanted to smack me with a stick. Fortunately, someone warned me in time. That young hero is here today. Do you know who it is?"

Cattail paused for a moment, and everybody looked around, wondering who it could be.

"The hero is none other than Acorn!" continued Cattail. "This dinner is in his honor. Come up here, Acorn, and give us a speech!"

Acorn sat still, stunned. All eyes were on him.

Surprised, Button looked at his friend and said, "Why didn't you tell me about this, Acorn?" Then, he smiled and nudged Acorn to get up.

Acorn stood, and broke out in a sweat. "Oh, dear," he muttered. As he made his way to Cattail, Acorn tried to think of something to say.

Looking out at the dinner guests, Acorn stammered, " I uh... I really didn't do any..."

Just then, something whizzed by Acorn's head, and a tiny cherry tomato hit a nearby tree with a splat! Then, another tomato landed at Acorn's feet. Acorn ducked and a third tomato bounced off Cattail.

There was silence for a moment, and then bedlam broke out. The frog jumped into the pond, the newts scurried to hide in the long weeds, and the finches flew to an overhead branch.

Out from behind a bush popped Walnut, holding a tomato.

"I thought I'd join your party and bring a dish to pass!" yelled Walnut. "How about some tasty tomatoes?"

With that, Walnut aimed the tomato at Acorn.

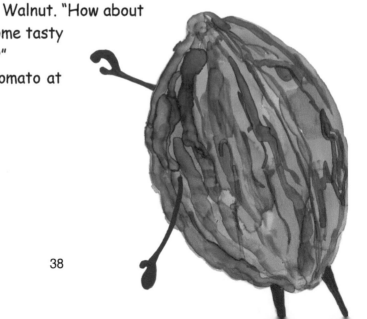

Button jumped to his feet, sword in hand, and shouted, "How dare you show your face around here, Walnut!"

Walnut turned and threw the tomato at Button instead. With great presence of mind, Button caught the tomato with the point of his needle, skewering it.

Meanwhile, the finches flew down to the napkin, picked up each corner in their beaks, and lifted it into the air. Plates, cups, raspberries, and juice spilled everywhere. The birds flew above Walnut and dropped the napkin right on top of him.

"Hey! Who shut out the lights?" Walnut cried.

Everyone watched as the bully thrashed around underneath the napkin. He stumbled twice and then fell. Breathing hard, Walnut lay still. The sound of muffled sniffling could be heard from under the napkin.

Acorn walked over to where Walnut lay and lifted one corner of the napkin. Seeing daylight, Walnut jumped up, shoved Acorn out of the way, and ran home.

"Why did you let him get away?" sputtered Button, "He ruined our dinner!"

"The dinner I took hours preparing in your honor," Cattail said, frowning.

Acorn pointed to a pile of tomatoes on the ground. Walnut had left them in his hurry to escape. "We could eat these," suggested Acorn. "Walnut said they were tasty."

Button nodded. "I wonder how they would taste roasted? I can skewer them and we can have tomato kabob."

Acorn and Cattail started a small fire while Button slid tomatoes onto his needle to roast. The finches put the napkin back in place. The frog and the newts returned. Everyone gathered the plates and they all feasted on cherry tomatoes in high spirits.

Button told tales of his adventures, Cattail shared a few etiquette jokes, and no one remembered Acorn's speech...much to Acorn's profound relief.

Just as dusk fell, the fireflies showed up at the party. They twinkled from every bush, adding to the festive air. When it was time to go, everyone thanked Cattail for his hospitality and they all set out for home, happy and full.

As Button and Acorn walked, Button remarked, "I must say that dinner went very well, in spite of Walnut's intrusion."

Acorn agreed. He glanced over at Button, and said shyly, "I've never had a friend like you before, Button."

Button gave Acorn a pat on the back. "And, I've never had one like you, Acorn. Ours is a friendship that has been destined."

Acorn wasn't sure what destined meant, but he smiled to himself all the way home.

About the Author

Laura Petrisin lived most of her life in New York before recently moving to the mountains of North Carolina with her husband and french bulldog. Retired from teaching, she spends a lot of time writing and painting with watercolors, oils and inks. Laura has illustrated several children's books and decided it was time to write and illustrate her own, beginning with Acorn and Button.

When not working, Laura often spends mornings at the backyard creek finding inspiration for story ideas.

Lightning Source UK Ltd.
Milton Keynes UK
UKHW051954130223
416963UK00002B/7